THE WINDIGO'S RETURN

A North Woods Story

BY DOUGLAS WOOD
ILLUSTRATED BY GREG COUCH

SIMON & SCHUSTER BOOKS FOR YOUNG READERS

To Kathy, Eric, and Bryan–
who explore the North Woods with me
—D. W.

To my wife, Robin, and my daughter, Emily
—G. C.

SIMON & SCHUSTER BOOKS FOR YOUNG READERS
An imprint of Simon & Schuster Children's Publishing Division
1230 Avenue of the Americas, New York, New York 10020
Copyright © 1996 by Greg Couch. Illustrations copyright © 1996 by Douglas Wood.
SIMON & SCHUSTER BOOKS FOR YOUNG READERS is a trademark of Simon & Schuster.
Book design by Paul Zakris. The text for this book is set in 15–point Lapidary Bold.
The illustrations are rendered in Acrylic and color pencil.
Printed and bound in the United States of America.
First Edition
10 9 8 7 6 5 4 3 2 1
LIBRARY OF CONGRESS CATALOGING-IN-PUBLICATION DATA
Wood, Douglas, 1951–
The Windigo's return: a North Woods story / by Douglas Wood;
illustrated by Greg Couch ; based on a legend of the Ojibwe (Anishinabe) people.
p. cm.
Summary: When the fearsome Windigo begins to prey upon the People of the
North Woods, a girl named Morning Star comes up with a plan to stop him.
ISBN 0-689-80065-7
1. Ojibwe Indians—Folklore. 2. Ojibwe Indians—Legends.
[1. Ojibwe Indians—Folklore. 2. Indians of North America—Folklore.
3. Folklore—North America.] I. Couch, Greg, ill. II. Title.
E99.C6W73 1996   398.2'089973—dc20 95-14832
CIP   AC

Author's Note

The Ojibwe term "Windigo" is still found throughout the Great North Woods, usually in place-names like Windigo Lake, Windigo Island, Windigo Road. But few people nowadays have any idea of what the name means. It was in the woods of northwestern Ontario many winters ago that I first heard a version of this delightful tale told by a white-haired Ojibwe (Anishinabe) woman. Since then my travels and readings have led me to many variations of the same basic theme, echoing through the ancient oral traditions of northern Native American cultures, from the East Coast to the Pacific Northwest.

Windigo tales often took place during the Winter Moons. This particular story employs a multi-seasonal approach.

Pronunciation Guide

ANISHINABE	ah-nish-ih-NAH-bay
MINI-GIIZIS	mih-nih-GEE-ziss
MANOMINIKE-GIIZIS	mah-no-men-EE-kay-GEE-ziss
MANOMIN	mah-NO-men
GITCHE-MANITO	gih-chee-MAN-ih-toe
WABUN ANUNG	WAH-bun AH-nung
KIWÉDIN	kih-WAY-din
ISKIGAMIZIGE-GIIZIS	iss-kee-gah-MIH-zih-gay-GEE-ziss

Once, long ago—
in the days of the Grandfathers—
something strange happened
in the North Woods,
the land of the Ojibwe.

It was a time when everything was good and the People had all they needed to live.

Summer brought *mini-giizis*, the Blueberry Moon. There was golden sunshine and just enough rain, so the berries grew plump and juicy. The fishing, too, was good, and no one went hungry. Later, as the nights turned cool, came *manominike-giizis*, the Rice-Making Moon. This was the time of the wild rice harvest, the gathering of *manomin*. Along the shallow shorelines the stalks were heavy with grain, and the People gathered it gently into their birch bark canoes. They offered prayers of thanks to *Gitche-Manito*, the Great Spirit.

No one could remember a better time . . . until one day, when something strange happened.

One of the hunters did not
return after spending all day
in the forest. Someone said,
"He has wounded a deer and
was tracking it down when
Grandfather Sun made his
evening lodge. In the
morning our hunter will
return, with much meat!" So
the people did not worry.

But morning came, and the hunter did not return. A woman went to the stream for water, and *she* did not return. Now the People began to wonder. Later an old grandmother went into the woods to gather firewood. She did not come back.

Now a dark fear crept through the village, like smoke from a dying campfire. The People gathered here and there in small groups and talked in whispers, pointing fearfully toward the forest. "Why are our People disappearing?" they asked. "What terrible thing is happening to our village?"

In one place the *white-hairs,* or elders, gathered. They had seen many winters, and their hair had turned white like the snow. As they talked of the disappearances, a white-hair named Waboose began to remember a story he had heard long ago, when he was very small. In the old story, people disappeared without a trace, never to be seen again. As Waboose talked, his memory became clear, and suddenly he *knew.* He knew that there was a *Windigo* in the forest and that the Windigo was eating the People!

A little girl named Wabun-Anung, Morning Star, was standing nearby. "My grandfather," she asked, "what is a Windigo?"

"A Windigo, my granddaughter, is a terrible giant of the forest," said Waboose, "and his ways are very strange. One of the strangest things about him is this. You might be out in the forest, sitting down or walking or gathering firewood, when you hear a sound: *T-R-R-O-M-P . . . T-R-R-R-O-M-P . . . T-R-R-R-O-M-P . . .* the great, heavy footsteps of the Windigo. You might turn around ver-r-r-y slowly to see what it is. Or you might turn around very quickly. But no matter how slowly or how quickly you turn, you will never *see* the Windigo.

"This is because he has the power to turn himself into anything he wants—a boulder perhaps, or a birch tree or an old stump. So you never know where the Windigo is—*until he has you!*

"And by then, Granddaughter, it is too late."

Morning Star listened with wide eyes, and her mind was full of questions, but words would not come. Waboose stroked her hair tenderly. "It is all right, Granddaughter. We will think of something," he said with a smile.

That evening the People held
a council meeting to decide what
to do about the terrible Windigo.
They sat in a circle around the fire.
Soon a warrior stood up. "We must
gather all our weapons," he said, "and go
out to do battle with this Windigo!" A
shout of approval went up from the People.
Surely all the warriors together could
defeat one Windigo.

But then someone remembered
that the Windigo could turn into
anything he wanted. It might not be so
easy to do battle with a tree stump, or a
boulder–especially if the warriors didn't
know which one to fight.

The People grew quiet.

Next, one of the white-hairs stood up. "This
Windigo knows where we live," he said. "Let us
move our village to a new place, far from here."
Everyone murmured and nodded their approval. But
then someone remembered that since the Windigo
already knew where the People were, he could just
follow them through the forest, capturing them and
eating them, one by one.

Again everyone fell silent. Not a word was said until, far to the back of the council-ring, a little girl spoke up. It was Morning Star. "I think . . . I think we should trap him," she said.

The People roared with laughter. What a fine joke that was, a little girl thinking of trapping a Windigo! But when the laughter died down, someone asked, "How would you do it?"

"We must go far into the forest," answered Morning Star, "and dig a deep pit. In the bottom of the pit we will place some venison, and all around the venison we will put birch bark and logs and sticks. Then we will cover up the pit with long grass and leaves, so the Windigo cannot tell it's there."

The little girl's idea made sense, and the next day the People did just as she had said. By nightfall the pit was ready. Everyone hid in the forest behind trees and bushes and waited for the Windigo to come. Deep in the middle of the night, when it was very dark, they heard a sound. *T-R-R-R-O-M-P* . . . *T-R-R-R-O-M-P* . . . *T-R-R-R-O-M-P.*

The Windigo was coming! Then another sound. *SNIFF, SNIFF, SNIFF, SNIFF.* He was smelling the venison they'd left in the pit. Or else he was smelling the People—no one could be sure.

Suddenly there was a great *C-R-R-R-A-S-H!*—and they knew they had caught the Windigo!

Quickly the People ran to the edge of the pit. Each one had saved a little glowing ember from the council fire. Now they threw the embers down into the pit, and the birch bark and sticks and logs began to burn. Soon a great fire was roaring in the bottom of the pit, and the Windigo began roaring too, screaming and howling in anger.

The People were frightened and ran back to their hiding places. Later, when it was quiet, they crept to the edge of the trap. They looked down, and there in the fiery pit was the Windigo! And he was furious!

"I'll get you all for this!" he roared, as he shook his great fist. "I'll come back again and again and again—and I'll eat you, and you, and you, and your children and their grandchildren, *forever and ever!*"

Terrified, the People fled once more into the forest. This time they waited a long, long, long, *long* time—until there were no sounds at all coming from the pit. Then finally they sneaked up, very, very slowly. They looked into the pit and saw . . . nothing! There was nothing there but a pile of ashes, all that was left of the terrible Windigo.

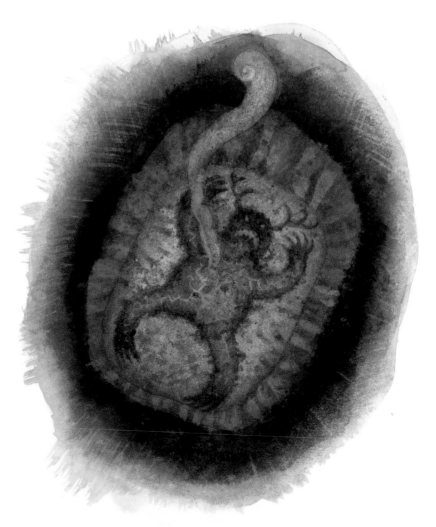

Still, the People remembered the awful curse of the Windigo and wanted to make sure he would not return to eat them all, as he had promised. "Gather the ashes," said Waboose, "and take them to the top of the high hill, where the night winds blow."

The People did as he said, and when they reached the top of the hill, they threw the ashes high up into the air. The night winds blew the tiny ashes, scattering them all over the North Woods. And the Windigo was no more, gone to the Land of Shadows.

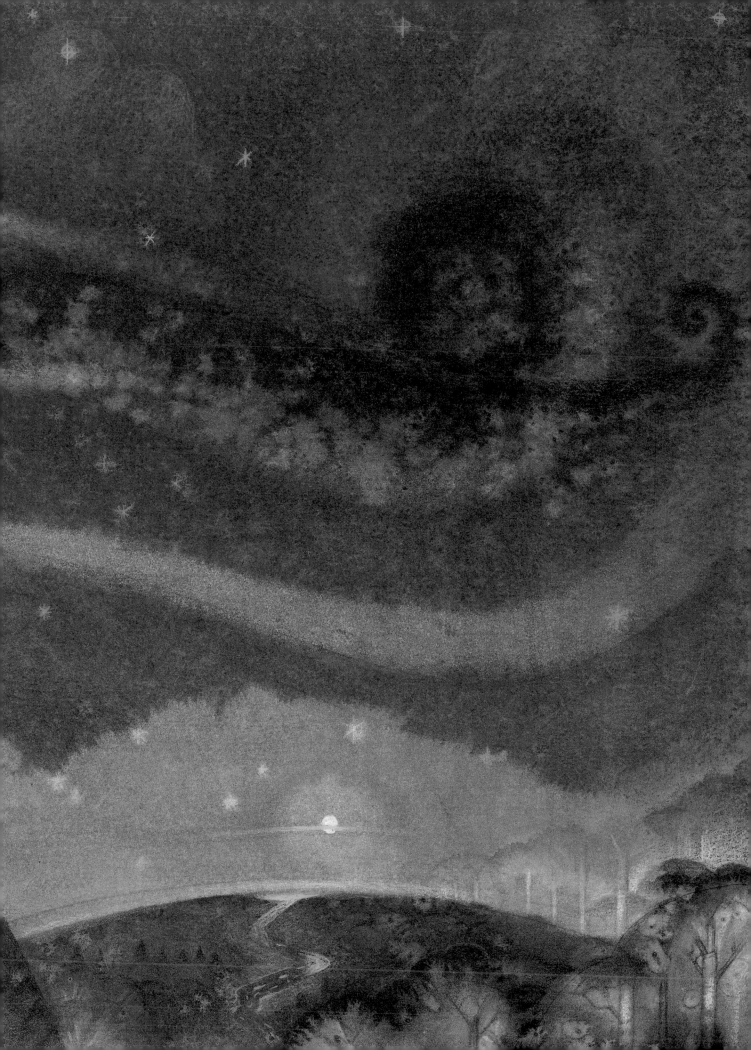

Hoa! The People breathed a great sigh of relief. They laughed and
shouted and hugged one another with happiness. They returned to their
village and began to live happily once more.

The autumn nights grew longer and the mornings white with frost, and the
People moved to their winter hunting grounds. The Windigo did not return.

Later, *Kiwédin,* the North Wind, came blowing his icy breath. Through the
long, cold moons, the snow piled in deep drifts, and the lakes froze like flat,
smooth stones. And the Windigo did not return.

Then came *iskigamizige-giizis*, the maple sugar time. This was a time of joy and feasting, as the People gathered together once more to tap the maple trees and celebrate the end of winter. Soon after that came the budding-seeds time and the warm blush of spring, the Flower Moon. The People planted corn and pumpkin and squash. And still the Windigo did not return.

In fact, the People had almost forgotten about the terrible Windigo. Then, one day in early summer, three of the People sat by a lake, fishing. It was Morning Star and her little brother, and Waboose, the old grandfather.

"Aaaa!" shouted Little Brother suddenly, and struck his arm.

"Oh!" cried Morning Star, and slapped the back of her hand.

"Aiee!" they both shouted, as they swatted themselves here and there.

Waboose looked closely, and he noticed something strange. Though there was no fire anywhere nearby, little ashes seemed to be floating in the air. The ashes drifted through the woods and gathered in a cloud around the three friends. When Waboose held out his arm, he noticed that the ashes were landing on his skin and *biting* him! And where the ashes bit, they left a little bump that itched and itched and itched.

It is the Windigo, Grandfather!" cried Morning Star. "He has come back!"

Waboose nodded. "Yes, my granddaughter," he said and smiled knowingly. "And I'm afraid he will be coming back every summer from now on and eating all of us, just as he said he would."

Waboose arose and took the children's hands. Together they turned down the path toward the village, to tell the People.

And so it was that the Windigo returned, and returns every summer
to this day, keeping the promise he made so long ago.